Honey, I'm Home

By

Janel J. Tutak

Strategic Book Publishing and Rights Co.

Strategic Book Publishing and Rights Co.
12620 FM 1960, Suite A4-507
Houston TX 77065
www.sbpra.com

ISBN: 978-1-62212-222-6

DEDICATION

Dedicated to my favourite sister for being this book's biggest fan since it was first written on loose yellow pages and throughout its stages of creation. Your continuous support and enthusiastic encouragement is, and always will be, greatly appreciated.

Also dedicated to all the men in my life, past and present, who aided in the creation of the character Thomas Beatrice. *jt*

CONTENTS

Janel J. Tutak

Chapter 1

HURRY HOME, KATIE

Music blasted from her car stereo. She tried to concentrate on the music, but wasn't succeeding. What did Tom mean by "please hurry home"?

The sound of his voice led her mind to imagine thousands of horrible things; reasons why he would need her to come home in that urgent voice. After five years of marriage, Katie learned that if Tom needed her to do something, she'd better do it.

Despite her worrying, she'd managed to calmly promise to be there twenty minutes tops. She winced, remembering his phone call had caused her to sign out of work four hours earlier than normal.

Katie Beatrice worked as a bookkeeper in the office her husband worked at. It didn't pay much, but she enjoyed the chance it gave her to get out of the house. And more importantly, it gave Tom the opportunity to check up on her. He worried about her a lot, so getting her the part-time job at Witco Insurance made sense.

Her fingers trembled as she turned the doorknob. The sun made the metal hot, and it almost burnt her hand as she opened it.

Slowly walking in, Katie felt her pulse quicken. A slate-grey paint welcomed her home as she entered the hallway. It wasn't at all warming. There was a wooden table by the door for keys and such. She set her purse down and tried to take deep breaths. *In and out. In and out.*

The hall led to each room—kitchen straight ahead, living room to the right. The staircase was farther down the hall to the left, as was the dining room, the bathroom, and a spare bedroom, which had been converted into a study. Cement steps led to the laundry room. Upstairs was their bedroom, another bathroom, and a guest bedroom.

She walked past the front hall closet, where their jackets hung neatly all in a row; perfectly measured, perfectly spaced. All their boots and shoes were likewise neatly set up.

"Hello, Tom? I'm home," she managed to squeak. Her voice echoed for a moment, then nothing. *In and out.*

The house was silent except for the sound of her heels clicking on the hardwood floors. She wasn't interested in this game of cat and mouse they played on a regular basis. She wandered from room to room, then climbed back down the stairs, her legs heavier with each step. Where was he?

His study? She wasn't allowed to go in there. But what if he was in there and needed her help? His phone call had sounded so critical, but was it worth it? What if he wasn't in there? He may become very angry. *In and out. In and out.*

No, she didn't want that.

She took her hand off the doorknob. "WHAT are you doing?" boomed a voice behind her. She spun around and came face to face with an angry Tom.

"I . . . I-I was . . ." she stammered.

"You were just snooping in my study!" he finished for her.

"No, it wasn't like that. You phoned . . . and I . . ." she tried to explain.

He slapped her face. "I know what I did! I thought you could help me, but I guess not!"

Tears stung her eyes; now she'd done it. Why couldn't she do anything right? She silently prayed the slap would be the end of today's fight. She barely heard his fierce words as he yelled. She held her arms against her body as she leaned against the wall. She couldn't bear to look at his disappointed face. She stared down at his feet. A familiar spot, a way to hide, to forget the pain. He wore his shoes in the house, as he always did. Italian leather. Everything had to be perfect.

Hearing her name screamed again, she glanced up, trying to wipe away tears. *Big girls don't cry!*

His expression changed, looking at her unhappy face. "Oh Katie, I'm sorry honey. I'm working on a surprise present for you, and it's not finished. Just think if you'd seen it! I'd be heartbroken." He paused, taking her hand. "Will you forgive me?"

"Of course," she mumbled. "I know I'm not supposed to be in there. I'm sorry—it's all my fault." Just like it was yesterday, when she broke his favourite glass. She should have waited till her hands were dry. She couldn't believe how careless she'd been; then again neither could he.

She gently felt the bruise on her thigh. It didn't hurt too much—*and after all*, she thought, *I deserved it.* It was his favourite beer glass. Her flashback was like a violent hurricane.

***

"My glass? Is that what just broke." She was silent as she'd bent down and fumbled to pick up the shattered pieces. "What the hell is the matter with you? I can't believe you'd be careless enough to drop my favourite glass! Do you even remember why it is important?"

Did he actually want me to answer? He'd slapped her, but she'd stayed in place. She didn't flinch. *Just pick up the glass and go to bed, Katie.*

"I won that last year at a Super Bowl party! Everyone in the office wanted it, but I won!" He'd kicked her in the leg like a football player kicks a field goal. "You were always jealous of that. I saw you eyeing it when I brought it home!" He'd kicked her again, this time hard.

She'd whimpered as the force caused her to jam a piece of the sharp glass into her finger. *What hurt worse?*

Then she was on her knees before him, like a servant to her master, and he was looming over her screaming. "Is that what I have living with me—a jealous bitch? I can't believe you!" She'd come face to face with his feet. Where were his shoes? There was a hole in his sock, and a gnarly big toe stared back at her. She'd turned away.

***

"Katie? Katie!? KATIE?!?" Tom exclaimed.

"Hmm? Oh sorry, yes Dear?" she stammered.

"I'm hungry. Could you make something please? Please Katie— no one makes a BLT like you."

Chapter 2

A BLT

A BLT? Is this what he called me home for? To make him a sandwich?

"Of course I will, Honey. Would you like your bread toasted?" she asked, even though she knew the answer would be yes.

Tom must have read her mind because he didn't answer—he only sat down at the table. She silently made him a sandwich. *I was really lucky today*, she thought. *I should have known better than trying to sneak into his study.*

Two slices of buttered, lightly toasted white bread. Not too crunchy, not too dark. Four slices of bacon cooked just so. Not too rubbery, but not so crunchy that they break and fall apart. Not pink— light brown. Fresh, crispy layers of iceberg lettuce. Not too many—*it's not a salad, Katie.*

Two medium slices of tomato. The little ones don't cover the bread, and the big ones hang out. Mayo on the top slice of toast, so that when it drips, it flavours the other layers of the sandwich.

Mayo, tomato, lettuce, bacon. *No one makes a BLT like me . . .*

She gave him the food and sat down opposite him, then nervously watched him eat. Did he like it? Was it good enough? A little bead of sweat drizzled down her face as she watched him devour the food.

"Milk," he said, spitting crumbs everywhere. As soon as the words left his lips, she leaped out of her chair. Her hands shook as she grabbed a glass. *Careful—don't break this one too.*

She poured the milk. He drank it all in one gulp and got up from the table. He didn't make eye contact with her and began putting on

4

his coat. She began clearing the table and cleaning up the frying pan. *Tom hates a messy house.*

She looked over at him. *Where on earth is he going now? Isn't he even going to say goodbye?* She had an overwhelming urge to cry but forced herself not to. *Tom hates when I cry. Big girls don't cry!*

"God, don't cry, Katie—you're such a baby sometimes. I have to go back to work. But I don't think we'll need you until next week." He called out before the door slammed. A chill ran up her spine as the sound lingered in the hallway.

Chapter 3

THE FACE IN THE MIRROR

Once he was gone, Katie could no longer stop the tears. She walked into the bathroom and tried to compose herself. She stood at the sink and looked into the mirror. The woman staring back at her was almost unrecognizable. She looked old and tired, not at all like the Katie she once knew.

Dark circles had formed under her eyes, signs of the sleep she no longer was getting enough of. Her mother always told her that worrying does nothing but make you age, and she was right.

Her makeup was smudged, and black mascara streaked her cheeks. Tears blurred her eyes and made her feel lost. She remembered a time when her eyes were happy and bright. How long ago was that? How did she get to this point in her life? Where had she gone wrong?

Katie grabbed a face towel and let the sink fill with hot water. She yearned for the warmth and wanted to get clean. The woman looking at her was ridiculous. She remembered another bathroom years ago.

She got out of the shower and reached for a towel. They were staying with Tom's brother and his wife until they found a place of their own. She stepped out and jumped as someone tried the door handle. *Nobody ever knocks*, thought the nineteen-year-old Katie. The doorknob rattled again. Then a loud knock against the door. Katie quickly wrapped the towel around herself.

"Yes?"

"Katie, open the door."

Oh—it was only Tom. "Just a second, I'm almost done drying off.

It sounded like he sighed. "Why do you have the door locked?"

"Because I'm in the shower." *Why wouldn't I have the door locked?*

"Katie, just open the door." She could hear his hand on the knob again. *Why is he so impatient?*

She grabbed the door to unlock it just as Tom was trying to open it. His force flung the door open wide and hard. It smacked her in the nose—CRACK!

"Ow!" she cried. "Tom I think you broke my nose!" The pain was unreal, and there was an overwhelming amount of blood.

He went to the kitchen and grabbed some ice. "Oops! I was just trying to get in. You shouldn't have had the door locked."

"But I told you it was locked!"

He threw the ice at her. "Forget it! I was only trying to help. You still shouldn't have had the door locked. What if there was a fire?"

His sudden anger surprised her. She said nothing, but began to cry.

"Steve and Joy were nice to let us stay, and look at the mess you're making, the floor—and Jesus, the towel!" She hadn't noticed the blood dripping on the towel and hoped it wasn't ruined.

He looked at her in disgust and walked away. Married only two weeks, and she was already pissing him off. She'd just have to try better.

***

Steam filled the bathroom, soon making the face in the mirror disappear. Katie wondered if someday she would too.

Chapter 4

SOMEONE'S BEEN SLEEPING IN MY BED

Katie was asleep when Tom returned home that night. She felt lonely, but hadn't wanted to wait up for him. She half-expected him to wake her when he got home, usually trashed, looking for some action. But not this time. Sometimes that worried her too. She wasn't sure what was worse. Was he too frustrated with her to care? Did he go elsewhere for companionship?

Another prostitute? It could happen again.

***

Tom stumbled into the bedroom after a night out with the boys. Is this where Katie's hiding? A good old game of hide and seek. He bashed his knee on the bedside table, disturbing his sleeping wife. "Tom is that you?" she said sleepily.

He slumped onto the bed. "Kaatieee, wake up," He said, slurring his words.

Katie rolled back over. "It's 2:30 in the morning, Tom. I'm going back to sleep."

He reached over for her and grabbed a breast. "Kaatieee."

"Not right now, Tom—I'm tired."

He tried again, this time the other hand grabbing lower, beneath the covers.

"I said no, Tom."

"Ssshhhh, now listen heeeerre, Wifey!" He didn't move his hands and fumbled around. "I'm the man, and I say yesss."

Katie sat up in bed. "No, Tom, not tonight. I'm going back to sleep."

His eyes seemed to glow in the dark as they became enraged. For a split second Katie considered giving him what he wanted. "What do you mean, *no*? Faacking woman, lisshen up. Yoooou've got to do what I shay."

He tried again, but with rougher hands. Now frightened, Katie tried to push his hands off her and screamed. He stopped for a second, and there was no sound in the bedroom but his heavy breathing. Then out of nowhere, whack—his hard fist against her arm.

Quickly Katie got out of bed. Her arm stung with pain, and she could barely lift it. "Tom, I can't be around you when you're like this. I'm sleeping in the guestroom."

He didn't have time to react, and she locked the door behind her. For a few minutes he banged on it and yelled. On the other side of the door, Katie was crying. Her husband's temper when he was drinking frightened her. He'd never been like this while they were dating.

What changed?

Katie sat in silence, waiting to hear his snoring from the next room. Her arm was throbbing; it was sure to bruise. She lay in bed for what seemed like forever, but it was only a few hours before she ventured out into her kitchen.

Concerned about waking a hung-over Tom, she decided to start some coffee. The scrambled eggs would wait until later, when she knew he was up for sure. *Tom hates cold food.*

But she quietly got out a pan to place on the stove. She would turn it off and on for a few minutes in hopes it wouldn't take long to get hot when he was ready.

She was pouring herself a glass of orange juice when she heard the bedroom door open, and then the sound of footsteps on the floor. The footsteps were oddly light, not at all like the trudging of a tired, half-drunk man.

Curious, Katie tiptoed closer to the hall, and ducked behind the wall. The bathroom door opened and Katie saw a bright pink nightie saunter back to her bedroom, the door closing behind it.

***

It could happen again.

Katie tried to keep her mind off it and worked out her frustration while she did her housework. *Man, Tom's a pig!* His stuff was all over the place. Crumpled collared shirts, wrinkled work pants, sweaty socks, tangled ties spread over their oak bedroom set.

The bedroom was so large it made Katie feel like a little girl. It was dark in colour and almost hard and cold, and it gave off the impression of a man's room. Dark curtains hung from the windows, keeping peeping eyes from looking in and the bright morning sun from creeping in. The sheets too were dark, and Katie's small, milky frame was lost in the thick comforter. There were no extra pillows—no frills, candles, or potpourri.

Katie didn't spend much time in the bedroom if she could help it. It was too dark for her. The only upside was, it didn't take long to make the big bed and move the clothes to the laundry basket, then down the hall to the laundry room to await laundry day.

The living room, on the other hand, was another story. Chip crumbs, beer bottles, and cigarette butts *oh my!*

And how I hate it.

Of course she didn't have the nerve to tell him how much. She didn't tell him anything about how she felt. It was too dangerous. Who knew what kind of a mood he'd be in. Besides, feelings were sissy stuff. Tom didn't care about feelings.

Today was Friday, so the whole house had to be cleaned—*and Tom hates a messy house.* And it was her job— to cook, clean, and to work part-time whenever he needed her at the office. She had to do whatever Tom needed her to do, and he had no problem telling her what that was.

The kitchen walls were white, and sometimes Katie spent hours scrubbing them. There could be no marks on the walls, the counters, or the floor. She knew better now than to trust her own eye. Tom could see better than her—he'd see the smudges on those walls from far away. She hated to disappoint him, so she listened carefully when he complained of something she'd done wrong.

She went to the bathrooms and made sure they sparkled too. No film on the shower door. No marks in the toilet, which wasn't easy when you had a husband who liked to get drunk and piss all over, but it had to be done. Towels folded on the rack, tags hidden, evenly lined up.

Next she moved on to the closets. Katie got out her ruler, she couldn't trust her eyes to make it evenly spaced. No she wouldn't make that mistake again. An inch and a half it had to be spaced. Between each hanger, an inch and a half, so each article did not disturb the next.

Although she was tired, Katie was happy to be at home and doing anything to keep her mind off things. She welcomed the times she had alone. And it wasn't that she didn't love him—*like a dog love its owner.*

But she was frustrated with herself around him, unable to please. She got a lot more done when he wasn't there, without him standing over her, making sure she did everything right, everything in its proper place. She was satisfied when it had only taken a few hours to clean.

Chapter 5

THE CAT CAME BACK

She didn't mind being lonely. When they first looked at the house, she imagined getting a cat or a dog to keep her company while Tom was at work. But when she'd mentioned something about it to Steve and Joy, she'd been warned it might not be the best idea.

"We had a few pets growing up, but they never lasted long." Steve had said with a laugh. "We couldn't stop them from running away, and it drove Tom crazy. After a while, Tom took to hunting our old cats down and using them for target practice with his pellet gun. Some of them got away, but not without a few injuries."

Katie remembered looking at him, waiting for him to admit he was just joking, but the conversation had ended and so had her dreams of getting a house pet.

After dark, she sat on the couch reading. Deep in her book, she hadn't noticed how late it was. Tom wasn't home yet, but she didn't pay much attention to that nowadays. Sometimes he felt like he needed to escape. It wasn't his fault she could get on his nerves. It used to worry her in the beginning, but now she understood his needs. The first time it happened, she was distraught.

***

They'd been married for only a few months, and he didn't come home from work for dinner. Katie sat at the table poking at the cold plate of food in front of her. By midnight she'd moved to the couch beside the phone. She called his work to see if he was still there and just working late, but there was no answer. She then started to panic.

She called the hospital, but there wasn't a patient to match his description. And the police station, but it was too soon to file a missing person's report. No one could help her, and she sat there waiting by the phone. She couldn't understand why things were over or what she'd done wrong.

A few days later, Katie had barely moved from her spot on the couch. Kleenexes lay around her from drying her tears, as well as empty food containers from the snacks on hand in the house. She'd barely eaten and hadn't showered, paralyzed with grief over the end of her marriage. She lived on the couch, incapable of even looking at the bed they'd once occupied together.

Tom returned home as if nothing had happened, as if he'd just come home after a day of work. At the sound of the door opening, she leaped up. *"Tom!"*

"What the hell happened here?!" he fumed.

She didn't pay attention to the words coming from his lips, so happy and relieved was she that he was home and with her again.

"Seriously, what the fuck, Katie? My living room is a mess. I see you've been lazy as usual!"

She reached out to hug him, yearning to feel the warmth and protection of his love. But he pushed her away wrinkling his nose, "Ewww, gross. What's the awful smell?"

"Tom, I missed you so much! Where have you been?"

His eyes grew dark like the skies before a thunderstorm. "Don't ever ask me that."

"Tom, I was so worried about you! I haven't see you for days."

"That's none of your concern," he snapped. "I'm not some dog on a leash that you can control. I'm a free man and I do as I please."

Katie thought back to what Steve had said about the family pets. Tom's shortness with her and his indifference about seeing her again made her feel ten inches tall.

"Clean up this bloody mess, would you? I'd like to enjoy the game in my own house. And for heaven's sake, take a shower would you?"

As if on autopilot, Katie scurried to tidy up the couch. She tossed the Kleenexes and food into the garbage and folded the blanket, and had a beer waiting for him on the coffee table as he plopped down in front of the TV. She then hurried to the shower. Even with his strange behaviour, she found she couldn't stop smiling. Her husband was home again, and all was right in her world.

***

Katie had learned not to worry when he disappeared and not to ask where he'd been. She knew he'd eventually come home, and he'd be in a better mood if everything was just how he liked it.

Chapter 6

A HOLE LOT OF TROUBLE

The next afternoon, the phone rang, "Hello?"

"Hey Babe." It was Tom.

"Hi, Hun."

"Peter and Bob are coming over for supper tonight. We have some business to go over," Tom explained.

"All right, yeah. Love you too. Okay, bye!" *Now I have to make something fit for his colleagues. I can't get away with pasta tonight, not without out a lecture.* Then she thought, *Business? Hmmm, what business? Peter and Bob don't work in his department.*

Just then a crashing noise interrupting her thoughts. Katie ran to the sound. It looked like the window had been left open. The door to Tom's study had swung open—and there was a hole in the wall. "Oh no!" Without thinking, she ran in to see the damage.

The knob had smashed a hole in the wall, and Katie had to tug hard to get it out. She felt like crying. Not only was he going to find out, but he was having company in that room tonight! Therefore it wasn't going to up to his standards, and it was going to be her fault.

She took a deep breath—*in and out.*

"I'll just tell him what happened," she muttered. The thought calmed her until she pondered it some more. How would she know about the hole inside the study, unless she was in the study!

What will I do? She rushed to the kitchen to prepare the meal for her guests. Maybe if the food was good enough, he'd focus on that.

The roast was in the oven when Tom came home from work. She kissed him hello and politely said hi to his colleagues, then went back to her work.

As Tom took Bob and Peter to his study, Katie held her breath. *Will he notice?* She pretended to set the table, and as she placed each utensil she kept her ears cocked.

Down the hall, Tom opened the study door and the men walked in. Then there was a pause before Katie heard whispering. *Bob or Peter must be pointing out the hole*, she thought.

She waited for Tom to yell her name. It was silent. *Why aren't they talking anymore?*

Then it came. "*Katie!*"

Katie's face turned pale, her arms broke out in goose bumps, and she suddenly felt faint, but somehow she managed to respond. "Y-yes?"

There was a long pause, and Katie tried to be brave.

"I'll have a Labatt," Tom called, then after a pause, added, "Okay—make that three."

Katie breathed a sigh of relief. "Coming right up, Dear!" Katie happily got the beers and walked towards the study and knocked.

"Come on in," Tom called. Shocked, Katie opened the door and set down the beverages.

"Thanks, Hun," he said while passing around the beers.

"No problem. Oh, and Honey? Dinner will be ready in five minutes," Katie said with a smile. She was relieved that for some reason the hole didn't matter, and everything was okay.

The guys exchanged glances, and Katie felt her cheeks turn hot. Bob cleared his throat and Peter turned away to look out the window. There was an odd pause and Katie felt like she should say something. "Will you be ready then?"

Tom gave the men a dashing look and rolled his eyes. "Katie, like I told you on the phone, we're going out for dinner to talk about business. No offence, Dear, but we're going to the newest hot spot in town, you understand? Sorry, Katie—we'll have to pass."

Katie was speechless—she'd spent hours on that meal! On his instruction! He'd said they were going to be here, she was sure of it! Unless . . . *was that last week?*

"Actually," he said, looking at his watch, "We better get going— we have reservations." Katie hardly noticed as they walked out of the room. Once again frustrated and stressed about her inability to listen, she just shook her head and sighed.

Honey, I'm Home

As Tom left the room, he poked his head back in the door. "Babe? There's a repairman coming at 6:30 to fix the hole in my study wall. Money's sitting out for you." he said before he left.

Maybe it wasn't me, she thought. She looked around the room and instinctively started to pick up the garbage on the floor. She was embarrassed Bob and Peter had seen the state of the study, but wasn't about to let that happen when the repairman came.

"My God this room's a pig pen! Thank goodness he never lets me come in . . ." Then her voice trailed off. "Hmmm. I wonder where my present is."

Excitedly she cleaned up the study, searching for her gift. At 6:15 the room was spotless and Katie still hadn't found it. She plopped into his chair and looked at the desk. The next thing she knew she was rifling around in his drawers.

"Aha!" she said, pulling out a big envelope with the inscription, "To my sweetheart, Love Tom." *Should I open it?*

"Maybe just a peek," she squealed opening the package. Her moment was interrupted when the phone rang. She jumped out of the chair and shoved the envelope back into the drawer before answering it. "Hello?"

"Hello?" It was a female voice. There was a long pause.

"Hello?" Katie repeated.

"Oh. Hi. Umm, is Tom around?"

"No—he's out at the moment. Can I take a message?" said Katie.

The woman's laugh was high-pitched. "Sugar, you can just tell him Judy phoned."

"Yeah, no problem. Does he have your phone number?" Katie asked. She grabbed a piece of paper and scribbled down the message.

Another laugh. "Oh, yeah—he's got it."

After hanging up the phone, Katie smiled when she found that the envelope contained plane tickets to Miami! *How romantic*, she thought. *I'll have to act surprised when he tells me!*

Chapter 7

FILLING A HOLE

Katie sniffed the air. *The roast!* she thought as she smelled smoke. It sent her back.

*****

"Katie, be a doll and do a beer run for me?" He was sprawled on the couch, watching football.

Katie looked up from the cutting board, where she was chopping vegetables. According to the timer, the meatloaf would be done in fifteen minutes. She hesitated, continuing to chop. "Do you mind if I go after dinner?"

"Katie, did you hear me? I asked you to go out and get beer. No later, not tomorrow—NOW!"

The sudden anger in his voice made her jump. The knife slipped and broke the skin on her index finger. "Shit!"

"*WHAT?*" She heard the couch move, as if he were getting up.

"Oh no—not you, Tom."

He sat back down. "Better not be."

She popped her finger into her mouth. Not too bad. It had stopped bleeding when she took it out.

"I don't hear you going to the door!"

She looked again at the timer. "Dinner will be ready in twelve minutes. I can't make it to the store and back in time to take it out."

"Oh my God, Katie! You're wasting time arguing with me. You could have been there by now!"

"Okay, okay. But will you listen for the timer please?"

"Just *go!*"

By the time Katie returned home, she knew Tom had been kept waiting an extra ten minutes for his dinner. If only the cashier had rung it up faster! She opened the front door and immediately heard the sound of the smoke detector. Fat had spilled over the pan causing the kitchen to fill with smoke.

Rushing with the oven mitts, Katie threw open the door and pulled out a blackened meatloaf, smoke pouring out. Coughing, she began to fan the smoke detector until the beeping stopped.

At the same time, Tom came out of his study. "What's that horrible smell?" He had a cigarette clenched in his lips.

"Dinner," she answered.

"It's burnt! What the hell—I'm not eating that!"

"Tom, I told you to listen for the timer!"

"I had to take a phone call. Besides, dinner is *your* job! Well done, Katie—you managed to mess that up too!"

His tone frustrated her and she became flustered. "*Me?* But you . . . so I—and you . . ."

"No Katie, not me—YOU! *You* burned the dinner!" He took his cigarette out of his mouth. "Hold out your arm."

She looked at him in disbelief. "*What?*"

"You heard me Katie—do *not* test my patience! Hold out your arm!"

Seeing his eyes deepen to a glaring black, she slowly did what she was told. He grabbed the milky white wrist so hard she thought it would break. "Do you like burned things Katie?" She shook her head. "*I can't hear you!*"

"No," she said meekly.

He stuck the cigarette into her forearm and she cried out it pain. He held it there for a few seconds. "Me either."

When he released her, she went to the sink and ran the water. The coldness numbed the pain for bit, but she could still feel it throbbing. She felt the pounding inside her head too—a headache coming on. She made sure her sobs were silent as she cried.

"Why isn't my beer in the fridge?"

***

19

Katie ran to the kitchen just in time to save her supper. She coughed in the smoke-filled kitchen. At least it hadn't caught fire—Tom would have a field day with that one. She looked down at the small scar on her forearm, a tiny lesson burned into her flesh forever.

The repairman should be here any minute. No use sitting down. She walked to the window and looked out, and saw an unfamiliar vehicle in the driveway. The doorbell rang and it startled her. She jumped and rolled her eyes with a smile as she opened the door.

"Good evening, Ma'am. Is this the Tom Beatrice residence?"

"Yes—I'm his wife, Katie. Please come in." She held the door open while the tall man walked in. She eyed him as he went.

He didn't exactly look like the type of person Tom would associate with. For one, his work shirt was salmon pink, and his pants were a tan colour. This man knew how to dress. Tom and his friends stuck with the basics: black, blue, green, brown, grey, white. And, well,—he had a bit of a sashay in his walk as he carried in his case. Katie's gay-dar went off. Tom and his friends would never hang out with someone who even *looked* like they might be homosexual.

Katie, on the other hand, felt comfortable with him. He wasn't exactly handsome, but she couldn't look away. He looked awfully familiar. Their eyes met and Katie blushed. "Is something the matter, Dear?" he asked.

Katie blinked back into the real world and realized she was just standing there. "No, sorry. The hole in the wall is this way." She led him to Tom's study.

"So how did it happen?" said the man.

She thought back to a little girl with pigtails at the grocery store that time. "Mommy, that lady's arm is all marked up," she'd said, pointing. "Hey, Lady—how did that happen?" As Katie had tugged on the sleeves of her sweater, the child's mother scolded the girl as Katie hurried out of the store.

"How did what happen? Oh, the hole? My husband must have slammed the door hard. I'm not sure actually," Katie answered.

"I see."

Katie went into the living room and read her book for a while. She stopped when a cough interrupted her. She looked up. "I'm finished."

"All right—thank you, Mr. uh . . ."

"Jack, Jack Green," said the repairman.

"Thank you, Mr. Green," said Katie.

"Please call me Jack."

"Okay, Jack. Wait a minute . . . Jack Green? From Oakbridge High?"

"Yeah, I went there. Wait—were you in Mr. Cambola's Home Ec class, senior year?" he paused while Katie nodded. "We worked on that quilt together. Katharine? Katharine Pegy?"

"Yeah, well I go by Katie Beatrice now. But it's me," she said with a smile.

He laughed. "Oh my God, what are the chances?"

"I know." She laughed. Then it dawned on her. "Hey—would you like to stay for dinner? My husband went out on business at the last minute and I have a whole roast, just came out of the oven," Katie said, giving her best sales pitch. She hadn't had a friend in a long time—not since . . .

***

"Who was that on the phone, Katie?"

Oh, just Lori. Some of the girls are getting together this weekend and she wanted to know if I wanted to come."

"Oh, dear." He sighed.

"What's wrong, Tom?"

"Oh, nothing really—it's just I can't believe that you still hang out with those silly girls." They'd all been friends in high school, taking a lot of the same classes.

"What do you mean? You used to hang out with them too," she said.

Tom tutted and shook his head, "Katie, Katie, Katie. That was in high school. We've grown up now, married. They're still gossiping about boys and looking at fashion mags. We're above that now—or at least I am . . ." He let his voice trail off. Tom always saw things in a way that Katie didn't and almost made it make sense. Needless to say, Katie was above those things now. The next time she'd hung out with those girls, she'd discovered he was right. They just didn't have anything in common anymore.

***

Jack's stomach growled. "Sure, I'd love to," he said with a smile.

"So how long have you been married?" he asked once they were seated at the table.

"Right after I graduated we dated for"—she paused—"about five months, and then he proposed to me. It's been almost five years now."

"Wow, that's so sweet," Jack said.

She always felt uncomfortable about discussing herself and Tom, so she changed the subject. "So what about you? Married? Single? Dating?" asked Katie.

"I just broke up with my boyfriend, George." He paused, his voice turning shaky. "We'd been going out for three years, and all of a sudden it just wasn't right anymore."

"Oh, I'm sorry," she said in a comforting tone. "I'm sure the right guy is out there for you somewhere."

"Thanks, Katie. That means a lot." He hesitated. "Why did we ever lose touch?"

Katie shook her head as she picked up the dishes. "I have no idea. I lost touch with everyone from high school, really."

Jack looked at his watch. "I hate to eat and run, but I have another job in an hour and I have to get ready. Thanks for dinner, though—it was excellent," he said as he got up.

"Oh of course, no worries. Here you go," she picked up the money Tom left on the counter and held it out to him.

But he shook his head. "This one's free of charge," he said with a wink.

"Thanks."

"Call me sometime—we can have coffee, okay?" he said, handing her a business card.

"I will, and next time I'll pay!" she said with enthusiasm. It excited her to have a friend. How long had it been since she'd done something with someone other than Tom? She thought back.

***

"Where are you off to dressed like that?" Tom had asked.

Katie looked up and caught the reflection of her husband in bathroom mirror. She was finishing applying her makeup and ignored the odd tone in his voice. "I told you—I'm going shopping with Nikki. She's picking me up in ten minutes."

"Is she even going to show this time?" He was smirking. The last time they'd had plans, Nikki hadn't called.

"Yes, Tom." Katie frowned. "We haven't seen each other in a really long time."

Katie stood at the door for a half an hour before she realized no one was coming. Tom gave her an amused look as she walked by with tears in her eyes. "I can't believe she didn't call or anything. Maybe I had the wrong day."

"Don't worry, Babe—I'm here. I'm all you're going to ever need." He put his arms around his wife. Nikki had called the night before and some how he hadn't gotten around to giving Katie the message.

***

After Katie closed the door she cleaned up the dishes and went to bed early. She had no idea when Tom returned from home because she was fast asleep.

Chapter 8

CONFESSIONS AND CONFRONTATIONS

The next morning when she awoke, Tom was gone. The weather was stormy and the house seemed gloomy, so she phoned Jack and asked if he wanted to have brunch. "Sure thing, Sugar. Meet me at Casey's at ten." She scribbled a note for Tom before running out the door.

Jack and Katie had a light meal and they spent an hour and a half catching up. Jack apologized that he had to work but promised he'd talk to her later. It was one when she strolled in the door.

"And just where have you been?" asked Tom.

"I was out—I left a note," Katie responded calmly. She kept a pleasant smile on her face as she walked past him.

"Your note said, 'I've gone out, be back soon, Love Katie.' "That doesn't really tell me much."

"I'm sorry, where was your note?" Katie said sarcastically.

"Don't talk to me like that," he said raising his hand. For a moment Katie thought he was going to hit her, but then his attitude changed. "So how was your evening last night?"

Surprised, Katie looked at him for a moment before replying. "Good. Watched *Jeopardy* and went to bed." She decided to leave out the part about rekindling a friendship with a homosexual high school friend. Over the years, she realized some topics were taboo. "Oh, and Judy called you." The colour washed from Tom's face.

"Judy called? The house?"

"Yes," said Katie without noticing, "I was in your study cleaning before the repairman came, and she phoned."

"Oh, she phoned my study line," said Tom, sounding relieved. "I'd better go call her, she's an important client." He got up and went into his study and shut the door.

Katie sat down on the couch reading. She cursed herself for egging him on like that. *I wonder what changed his mind.* She shrugged, thankful he hadn't left her a souvenir or two.

She was in a surprisingly good mood while she fixed them an early supper. She waited for Tom to say something, but he didn't speak. After she cleared the dishes, she went back to her book. Tom sat at the table for a while longer, then went into the bedroom and came out with a suitcase. Katie watched as he then went into his study and came out with the envelope.

Her heart leaped! She pretended to be reading. *Act surprised*, she told herself, *just remember to act surprised.*

"Katie."

"Mmm?" she replied, not looking up from the novel. *Smooth*, she congratulated herself, *just play it cool.*

"Can you come her for a minute?" he asked in a tone that was more like a command.

Puzzled by his tone, Katie put down her book and walked into the front hall. "Yes, Tom?" Perhaps it was for a better surprise effect. That must be why he hadn't hit her earlier either—to keep her guessing.

"I have to go on a business trip for a little while. I'll be back in a couple weeks or so," he said.

Katie's jaw opened, then she closed it. Maybe he didn't want to tell her yet. "You're going alone?" she said, fixing her hair.

"Sorry, Katie—I can't take you on this one. Six tickets to Miami is about all the company can handle. Another six for everyone's spouse, it's too much. You'll have to stay behind," he said with his serious face.

Maybe he wasn't joking. Maybe she wasn't going. He was really going to leave her behind! If she wasn't his sweetheart, then who was? Her mind was racing. "But the envelope said, 'To my sweetheart.' That's me!" she blurted out.

Tom dropped his suitcase and slapped her. "You were snooping in my study again!" he boomed. He picked up his bag and started to leave.

"But, Tom!" said Katie, crying. "I don't understand!"

He hit her in the head with his suitcase and she fell to the floor. "Now do you understand, Katie? I'm going on a business trip and you can't come!" He was screaming now. "When will you learn that I have to support us by working? I can't always be babysitting you!"

Katie barely heard him screaming. His words were fuzzy and faded in and out. She opened her mouth to say something, but couldn't find the words. *Why is he still yelling at me?*

He walked over to her. There were those shoes again. Didn't he ever clean them? There was green gum on the sole of the right one; spearmint, his favourite kind. She saw his mouth moving but no sound. Then everything went pitch black.

When she awoke, she was blinded by bright lights. She blinked back, trying to adjust. The strong scent of disinfectant slapped her in the nose. She tried to sit up, but an agonizing pain struck her like a bolt of lightening. She reached up to the sore spot, moaned, and lay back down.

"Oh, sleeping beauty awakes," said a friendly female voice. "You should lie still." The woman pushed a button. "The doctor will be with you in a moment."

Doctor? Where am I?

"I'm Jess," the woman said. "If you need anything, just let me know."

"My head hurts," Katie said with a groan.

The nurse chuckled. "I'm not surprised. You have a concussion."

A concussion? She lay back and closed her eyes until she felt a new presence.

"Good afternoon—I'm Dr. Nobast," he said, looking up from his chart, "So, Mrs. Beatrice, how are you feeling?"

"My head hurts," she repeated as her stomach grumbled, "and I'm hungry, I guess."

Dr. Nobast and the nurse laughed. Jess glanced at her watch, "The food cart will be coming by soon. When you eat, you can take these pills to get rid of that pain."

"So I have a concussion?" she said, wincing as she sat up.

He nodded. "Do you remember how it happened?"

Honey, I'm Home

Katie looked like she was trying to recall something from a long time ago. Nothing came to her and she shook her head. "Not really, no. I forget what I did yesterday," Katie confessed.

The doctor and nurse exchanged smiles. "Well, perhaps we can help with that bit. Yesterday you slept for most of the day. We tried to wake you every now and then, but you were on medication and apparently very tired. You've been unconscious since Friday," said Jess. Katie glanced around the room, looking for a calendar. "Today's Monday," the nurse supplied for her.

"Thanks—I forget what I did at all Friday," Katie said as she heard movement in the halls. She tried to look out.

"The food carts," said the doctor. Katie nodded, her stomach rumbling again.

"We'll leave you to eat, but if you—" the doctor started, but a knock interrupted him.

"Hey, Sugar. You allowed visitors?" It was Jack. Katie looked over at the hospital staff and they nodded in acknowledgment.

"Come in," Katie invited, but he was already inside and pulling up a chair.

Dr. Nobast and Jess left quietly.

Chapter 9

VISITING HOURS

"So, Hun, how're you feeling?" asked Jack as a woman walked in with a tray, which she set in front of Katie. She smiled at Jack and left the room.

Katie said to Jack, "My head hurts a lot. I've got an unbearable headache."

He got up and closed the blinds, shutting out the blinding sunlight. When he didn't come back and sit down, she looked up at him.

"I was so worried. I called your office looking for you, and they told me you had an accident and were in the hospital. But when I got here, they would only let family members in. I had to wait until you woke up, to see you. It was awful."

She smiled. "I'm fine, really I am." She paused chewing on her lip. "So I had an accident?" He looked at her puzzled. "I don't remember what happened at all," she explained.

He nodded. "Yup. You fell down the stairs, Tom found you at the bottom."

Right—Tom! Where was he anyway? She longed for his warmth.

"Katie, you had bruises and red marks all over your body. Now I know they say you fell down the stairs, but . . ." *But what? What's he getting at?* "Well, I don't know. Its just I can't picture you falling down the stairs in high school," he said.

"Well, I am more clumsy lately, but there's nothing wrong with that. What are you getting at, Jack?" she asked.

"Just that . . . maybe it was no accident," he answered.

"What? You . . . you think . . . you think Tom did this?" Katie said angrily.

"Well, I don't know . . . yeah," he said, turning away from her confused eyes.

She sat there in shock, and he could see the words hurt. Finally she spoke: "Tom loves me!"

Jack glanced down at her tray of food—she hadn't touched a thing. "I'd better go—you should eat. It's good to see you," he said with a slight smile.

"He loves me, Jack—he does!" But Jack didn't hear her because he'd left.

Now it was her turn to stare at the food. She had a bite, then forced herself to get the tasteless food down her throat.

A nurse came back later to collect the tray. "I'm glad you ate all the food. Most patients don't," she said with a laugh as she walked out the door.

Katie sat in her room, motionless. How dare Jack accuse Tom of putting her in the hospital? Sure he slapped her a few times, but nothing serious, and only when it was her fault! If only she wasn't so stupid, if only she wasn't so careless. Oh, well, it didn't matter. She could never believe he'd thrown her down the stairs. She felt nauseated and dizzy. She slumped back down in her bed and napped till dinnertime.

The cart was screeching down the hall again, finally stopping in front of the door. But she didn't move. Someone came in and set down her tray. But she didn't budge. The nurse looked over at her, shrugged, and left.

Katie didn't feel like eating. She just sat there thinking. When the nurse returned to collect what should have been an empty tray, she was disappointed that Katie hadn't even tried anything.

Jess walked by and the two nurses whispered something Katie couldn't hear. Jess nodded and walked in and sat on her bed. "You didn't touch your food, Hun. Is there something else I can get you?" she asked. When Katie just shook her head, Jess said, "That man who came by earlier, was that your husband?" Again Katie just shook her head.

"Oh, sorry," said the nurse, then paused, probably expecting Katie to say something. "He was here at least four or five times a day, so I just assumed."

Katie didn't answer, but she was mad at Jack, not Jess.

"All right—we'll leave you then," Jess told her.

"Thank you. I just want to be alone for a while," she said.

Jess looked hopelessly at the other nurse, then left the room. They shut the door and Katie closed her eyes. Not a minute later the door opened again. *Don't they know what leave me alone means?*

"Hello, Katie." She recognized his deep masculine voice but did not turn to see the face. He walked over to the other side of the bed, forcing her to see him. He had tears in his eyes. "Oh Katie . . . when I saw you on the floor like that, I nearly died. I didn't know what to do!"

"Where have you been, Tom?" she asked coldly. That caught him off guard, and he was too stunned to answer. "Jack was here several times. Where were you?" she asked again.

"Jack?" Tom's eyes darkened like the sky before a storm, "Who the hell is Jack? Have you been fooling around on me Katie?"

Katie caught her mistake right away. "No no, Tom I'd never do that. It was Jack Cine from high school, don't you remember him?"

"Oh that queer."

"Please don't talk about him like that, he's my friend. And you're changing the subject, he came to see me but where were you?"

"I'm sorry I couldn't be here every second, but I had to work. Life goes on, Katie, and there are bills to pay. If I'd been here, how would we afford our house?" She stared at him in disbelief. "And I was in shock. It's not everyday I come home to find my wife on the floor, unconscious. It was hard for me to come see you, because whenever I was on my way over here I'd panic and see you lying there on the floor. I tried my hardest to block out the memory, but then when I thought that you may have . . . well, you know. I thought maybe if I'd found you sooner, or hadn't stayed at the office so late. I'm really sorry Katie," he said dramatically.

She bit her tongue for speaking to him like that. After all, he had saved her. She could have been worse off. "Don't worry anymore, Tom—I'm fine," she said, changing her tone.

"I can't bear to see you in a hospital. When do you get to go home?" he asked.

"I just need to keep her under observation tonight to make sure she's okay, then she can go home," said the doctor, who'd just come through the door. "I'm sorry, Sir, but visiting hours are over. You can come back tomorrow and, if all goes well, take her home."

"Thanks, Doc. I'll see you tomorrow, Babe." He leaned over to kiss her, but she turned away. Embarrassed, Tom hurried out.

"I heard you didn't eat any dinner. Are you feeling okay?" asked Dr. Nobast.

"Oh yeah, I'm okay now. I was just worried that Tom hadn't come yet. I'm fine," Katie lied.

"All right then—I'll see you tomorrow. Sleep well."

But she couldn't sleep. She tossed and turned. Awful dreams haunted her until she woke with a start. She had an unpleasant nightmare. In it she had found out Tom had been cheating on her, and then they had a fight. Tom had hit her in the back of the head with his suitcase. "It seemed like déjà vu," she said aloud. Then she gasped as the pieces fell together. It really happened!

Chapter 10

THE TRUTH, THE WHOLE TRUTH

The next day Katie threw up. Sure Tom had hurt her before, but not like this, and not on purpose. He just had a bad temper and she could bring the worst out in him by screwing up. But all that was minor. Never had he put her in the hospital. Everything came back to her now—the phone call from Judy, the trip to Miami, the fight. Now she was dizzy from the stench of her own stupidity.

When the nurse brought in her breakfast tray, she forced herself to eat the overcooked eggs and burnt toast. When Dr. Nobast came in to see how she was, she tried her best to look happy. In the evening, Tom came to pick her up and signed the release forms.

She didn't dare look at him as he drove, for the fear of upsetting her stomach once again. He was silent on the drive home, as if he understood how she was feeling. But how could he? He was acting as if he was some big hero, saving her from the floor where she lay in her own puddle of blood. And she'd bought and sold his whole I-was-in-shock story!

When they stepped inside, Katie immediately saw the house was spotless. "Katie, I hired a maid to clean the house as a way of apologizing," he said, kissing her neck. She melted into his arms.

That night, as he made love to her, she whimpered. "Don't worry, Katie—Tom is here now." She lay there frozen. She didn't understand. She loved Tom and thought he loved her. But he didn't care about her feelings, Jack did. He was a real friend. Right then she decided that she was going to tell Jack *everything*.

He was watching TV when she phoned. "Jack, I'm so sorry. I didn't mean to be so rude, I just didn't want to hear what you were saying to me. Want to go for coffee? My treat?" Katie begged.

Jack giggled. Of course he forgave his friend. "I'll be at Tim Horton's in ten minutes."

"Tom, I'm going out for coffee, okay? Do you want me to bring you back anything?" Katie asked after she hung up.

"No thanks, Dollface, I'm going to work soon and won't be back till late. I'll eat out, so don't worry about dinner tonight. You just rest up." She waved goodbye as she walked out the door.

"That's awful, Katie," cried Jack, his eyes filled with tears as he stared in astonishment. They were sitting in a booth and Katie had just told him everything about the abuse, the cheating. " How can you live like that? You need to leave him, right away."

Katie paused for a moment, sipping her coffee. "I can't, Jack—it's too hard." She looked out the window. The thought of the family pets entered her mind again. "Besides, he'd never let me go. I'm positive he'd come after me—that is, if I made it out alive . . ." She let her voice trail off.

"Don't even talk like that! Make sure Tom's not there. Just pack up your clothes and leave," said Jack, clasping her hand.

"I . . . I can't. Where would I go? How would I live alone, after all these years? I just can't," she said, making excuses.

"You can stay with me. You'll be safe there, and we'll get a restraining order against him," said Jack. Katie nodded as she finished her coffee. "Everything will be all right."

He did paint a nice picture—freedom. She sighed. "Okay, but I'd better get going, I think. Well, he's at work today, working late, and maybe . . ." she glanced down, blinking back tears. She couldn't force out the words. *Jack's right—it was for the best. Tom's hurt me for the last time.* "Thanks for the talk, I'll, um, I'll see you at your house."

They stood up and Katie paid. Jack gently hugged her bruised body goodbye and they parted. Her hands shook as she drove home. When she pulled into the driveway, she was relieved to see Tom's car wasn't there. She immediately went to her room and started to pack.

Katie reached under her bed, pulling out her big brown suitcase. Her nerves got the best of her. She reached for the phone and called Jack. "I can't do this," she blurted out.

"Katie?" asked the voice on the other end.

"Yeah, it's me," she said, sitting down on the bed.

"What do you mean, you can't do this? We discussed it. All you have to do is pack your things and leave," Jack said. He made it seem so easy to do. Could it really be?

"No—it's harder then that. I just can't!" Katie cried.

"Sure you can, Hun. Do you want me to come over?" he asked. *Why am I such a baby all the time? Big Girls Don't Cry!*

***

Katie sat in the corner, overwhelmed by tears. She held the spot on her arm where a purple welt was already forming.

"Katie, would you stop crying? I'm trying to watch the game!" yelled Tom from the couch. She wanted to stop, but it hurt. Why didn't he love her? Why couldn't she do anything right? "Seriously, Katie— shut up. You sound like a wild dog. What's the matter with you?"

"Tom, you really hurt my arm," she wailed.

"Oh, please. I barely touched you!"

"Then why do you think I'm crying?"

He leaped up from his seat. "Do you know why you're crying, Katie? *Because you're a big baby!* You cry to get things you want! I'm watching my game so you can't have my attention, and now you're crying when all I did was tap you. *Well, I'll give you something to cry about!*" Then he slapped her.

"Ow Tom—don't!" she cried.

"Then SHUT THE FUCK UP!" He lost it and kicked her a few times. "Big girls don't cry, Katie! Big girls don't cry!" He repeated it over and over, beating her as he said it. *"Big girls don't cry!"*

***

Big Girls Don't Cry.

She sniffed back the tears. "No, I'll be all right. I'm coming right over." She wiped her cheeks dry. "Thanks, Jack . . . for everything," she said before hanging up.

Katie sighed, then resumed packing. Soon she'd be at Jack's house, safe. Soon she wouldn't have to worry about anything ever again. Tom would be long gone and she'd be okay.

"Honey, I'm home!"

Chapter 11

HONEY, I'M HOME

Katie froze at the sound of his voice—he was supposed to be at work!

"Katie?" he called from downstairs. She remained motionless in the bedroom. Perhaps he wouldn't hear her. But it was like he had radar. She heard his footsteps on the stairs. One, two, three. It was as if her breathing both quickened and stopped as he got closer. Four, five, six. She heard him call out again. "Katie, are you up here?" It was like a game of hide and seek . . . or cat and mouse.

"Oh, there you are," Tom said, walking into the bedroom. Pouncing on his prey. She turned and smiled weakly at him. His eyes turned black as he glanced over at the stuffed suitcase on the bed. "Where are you going, Katie?" he demanded, taking a step closer. "Are you planning on skipping town, Katie?" His face reddened and his voice grew louder. "Were you planning on telling me, Katie?" With every word he got closer and closer. Katie couldn't move or speak.

"What's wrong, Katie? Huh? KATIE!?" he said, pushing her back. Tom let a smile spread on his lips as he watched her fall. The motion caught her off-guard and she screamed as she fell back, knocking over a vase of flowers.

"Tom . . . just calm down," she pleaded as she lay on the floor. "I . . . I'm just going to my parents for a bit," she tried to explain quickly.

He laughed a cold laugh that sent chills down her spine. "Really? For some strange reason I don't believe you." Her face grew hot as he continued: "For one thing, you seem to have packed stuff for all seasons, and for another, your mom called, asking about you." He laughed.

Katie didn't answer. *Why is he laughing? Does he know what's going on? Maybe he's really lost it this time.*

"Obviously your mother wouldn't ask how you are if she's going to see you soon," he went on. Again Katie said nothing. *He's right. What will I do now?*

"What's the matter, Katie?" he asked, egging her on.

"I'm leaving you," she squeaked out.

"You *what*?" he yelled.

"I said I'm leaving you Tom," she repeated, a little more bravely this time.

"Like hell you are. After all I've done for you? You ungrateful bitch," he hissed. "I provided you a house, food, clothing, and this is how you repay me? I don't think so!" He was screaming now.

What happened next was all in a blur. Suddenly Tom had his hands around her neck, and she tried screaming but no sound came out. Then he was bashing her head against the floor, and she heard the loud thumps and felt the shards of glass from the vase. In a terrified panic, she grabbed a large piece of the thick glass and stabbed him. Blood squirted her in the face, but his hands remained around her neck, so she stabbed him again, still screaming. More blood gushed out. Again, and again she stabbed, until Tom's hands let go of her neck.

Katie grabbed her stuff and ran down the stairs, not turning to look at the body on the floor. She ran on, not even locking the door. It was a mad dash to her car, and she threw her suitcase in the back seat. Then she hopped in behind the wheel and started the engine.

Katie drove like a maniac. She was lucky there were no cops around to stop her. Even if one had tried, she wouldn't have slowed down. She was driving straight to Jack's house, not even wiping the blood from her face.

She was in pain but was unable to cry out for help or speak. As if she were frozen, she kept going. She had only one thing on her mind—getting to Jack's, to safety. And when she got there, she banged furiously on his door.

"I'm coming," he called, but she continued to knock. Her brain just told her she needed to get inside, to Jack. "Wait a second—I'm coming," he repeated, chuckling.

But when he opened the door, there was blood-splattered Katie, her hair a mess and her arms bruised. "My God, Katie—what happened?" She didn't answer, just passed out on his doorstep.

Honey, I'm Home

When Katie came to, she was on the couch. She opened her eyes and felt a cold compress on her forehead. "Katie, are you okay?" asked Jack. She blinked back the sunlight and looked around. "You're in my living room. Katie, are you okay?" he repeated.

She sat up and stared at Jack's concerned face, "I'm okay."

"Do you need to go to the hospital?" She shook her head. Jack breathed a sigh of relief. "You really had me worried. What happened to you?"

"What do you mean. Oh. Sorry I was late," she said looking down at her bloody clothes. "Oh my God. Tom!"

"Shh. Just lie still—I'll get you some tea," he said, getting up. Katie just sat there in horror, the whole fight coming back to her.

"Sugar and milk?" he asked from the other room.

"Mmm? Oh yes," she replied absently.

He came out and set down the tea. "Katie, don't worry. Tom can't hurt you now."

She gave him a grim smile. "Oh, Jack—you have no idea how right you are."

"What do you mean?" he asked, puzzled. She just took a sip of her tea. "Katie? Hun? What happened?" he asked again.

"Nothing, Jack. Well, it's just that he came home while I was packing. I told him I was leaving him," she replied. Jack stared at her for a minute, then smiled, "Did he tell you the best of luck?"

She shook her head. "No—this is serious." His grin disappeared, of course it was. Look at her.

"Sorry, I'm listening. What did he say?"

Tears streamed down her face, and she shook her head again. Jack waited for her to answer. She sniffed. "It was more like where did he hit first." She took a deep breath. "We got in a fight."

Jack passed her a tissue, "Are you okay, Katie? Are you sure you don't need to see a doctor?"

"No, Jack—I'm okay now." She took another sip before continuing. "But he was choking me and I . . . I couldn't breathe. I thought I was going to die. He broke a vase and the glass was in my hair and, oh I was so afraid," she explained.

"Katie what are you trying to say?" he asked cautiously.

"I stabbed him. He's dead," she said bluntly.

Chapter 12

PLAN B

Now it was Jack's turn to be silent. "Well say something, please—anything," she begged.

"Did you check?"

"Did I check? Umm, no. I didn't, but I don't know. There was a lot of blood, and he wasn't breathing," she said, bursting into tears. "Jack, I don't want to go to jail. I didn't mean for this to happen. I was just afraid, and—"

"Katie, don't dare think for one second this is your fault," he interrupted. "If anything, that bastard had it coming, it was self-defence."

They hugged while Katie calmed down. Then they sat in silence, drinking their tea. "Jack, do you really think it was self-defence?" she asked doubtfully.

"Of course I do. He was abusive, for gosh sake—he put you in the hospital," he replied quickly.

"And look at the marks on your neck," he added.

Katie nodded. That part was true, but . . . "I didn't press charges. No one has seen him hit me, and I've never told anyone but you," she pointed out. "It's hearsay."

"True," he said slowly. The law wasn't always fair in cases like this. "I don't know what else there is for you to do then. I guess you'll have to run away," he said with half a laugh.

Katie looked at her friend with a straight face. "Exactly."

Jack should his head. "I wasn't serious. You can't run away. a friend of mine named Dorothy tried running away once, didn't work so well for her. There's no place like home."

Honey, I'm Home

"But what is a home? My 'home' isn't the same place I thought it was. I'll take Oz any day," she said softly.

"Then you'd better take your Scarecrow with you. Don't shake your head at me, Katie—my mind's made up."

He stood up and held out a hand. "To Oz?"

Katie reached out to his hand. "To Oz." The moment felt cheesy and yet made her feel better. Then Jack took out his car keys. "Where are you going?" she asked.

"Never mind. I'll be back in a flash—just going to the store. Stay here and don't answer the door, just in case," he instructed.

When Jack left, Katie looked around. A little nervous, she locked the door, then took her time as she walked into his bedroom. She began to realize what she was about to do—and what she was asking Jack to do. *This is wrong.* She decided not to pack his things after all.

Chapter 13

TIME FOR A CHANGE

Jack returned and handed her a small drugstore bag. "What's this?" she asked.

"Just look inside. It's something to help you," he replied. Puzzled, she peeked in the bag. There was a box in it, and when she pulled it out she realized what it was. Shocked, she shook her head.

"And people tell me I'm a drama queen! Calm down, Katie. Since they'll be looking for you, this is the only way we can hide you," he reassured her. "It's important."

"But my hair, my beautiful hair. I've never dyed it before," she stammered. But she had changed her hair, once . . .

***

Katie sat in the chair at the hair salon, watching her hair falling about her. Snip, snip, snip. The weight off her shoulders felt nice. She was tired of her long hair and needed a change. In no time, six inches of her long blond hair was being swept off the floor. She drove home feeling quite happy with the new style. It had been ages since she'd done something new.

Katie couldn't stop smiling as she walked up to the door. "Honey, I'm home!" she cheerfully called into the house. Tom was sitting on the couch watching TV. "How was your day?"

He didn't look up at her. "Fine." Sensing he wasn't feeling talkative, she started dinner.

Later, as they were eating, he said, "You cut your hair."

Instinctively, Katie put her hand to her new do. "Yeah."

"It's going to take a long time for it to grow back."

She lowered her hand and shook her head. "I don't want it to grow back."

"Oh." He was silent for a while, but before he got up he added, "Too bad. You used to have nice hair. Why would you change it?"

***

Jack was right—it was important, so they wasted no time applying the colour to her hair. She watched as her once-blond locks turned brunette.

Katie sat looking at the mirror. The women staring back at her was unrecognizable. Who was she now? Running away from her problems, afraid to share her fears and true feelings to people who were only there to help her, running away from her job, leaving her life behind. She wasn't the same person she used to be. Now she was a frightened woman who'd committed murder.

"Jack, I'm going to miss you. But I've thought it through. There's no reason for you to go." His eyes widened as she went on. "You have a life. I don't want to be responsible for destroying it."

Jack stared at her in disbelief and astonishment. "Katie, you aren't destroying my life. There isn't much this town has to offer me. I'd be much happier if I was with you. Protecting you," he said.

"That's very generous of you, Jack. But I don't need someone to protect me anymore. He's dead. I killed him. *I'm* responsible. Not you—me. I have to start living my own life. I can't let you ruin your life for me," she said firmly.

Jack opened his mouth to object, but Katie cut him off. "Like I said, I've thought about it. Nothing you can do or say can change my mind. You're safer here."

There was an awkward silence. Finally Jack nodded and walked to the door. Katie stood up, wiped the tears from her eyes, and walked over to her friend. "Please don't resent me for leaving like this. I'd love to take you with me, but I have to do this on my own. I have to find out who I am. I'm so sorry."

"Sugar, I'll never resent you. I think I understand what you mean," he said, giving her a big hug. "Goodbye."

"No, not goodbye. Just farewell, for a little while anyway. I'll keep in touch. I just need to settle in," Katie said. "Need to let all this settle down. When I'm safe, I'll get in touch."

She kissed his cheek, before exiting and getting in her car. When the door slammed shut, she started her new life—*alone*.

Chapter 14

A NEW LIFE

Katie watched the familiar town disappear behind her as she drove to freedom. She passed the hospital, the coffee shops, the diners. She drove past her work and the grocery store—all the familiar sights she'd never see again. It was all the past now.

She passed the sign that said, "Thank You for Visiting the Town of Oakbridge." "Goodbye," she whispered as she pressed the gas pedal harder and drove on.

For hours she drove from town to town. She didn't really know where she was—or where she was going, for that matter. All she knew was that she had to get away and fast. Who knew how long it would take the police to find Tom's body. *No, don't think of that—you have to think positive!* This was a chance to start over.

Later that afternoon, Katie pulled into a gas station. While the tank was filling, she checked her surroundings. She was in a small town, probably the type where everybody knows everyone. Tom would have hated it here. *Who cares what he thinks! You're a new person now.* "My name is Kathy Pegy," she whispered over and over to herself.

"Hello there, Sugar!" said a cheerful voice. Now Kathy in her mind, she looked over at a tall, older woman filling her tank. Her curly red hair was in a messy ponytail. Kathy smiled back at the cheerful face. The woman said. "My name's Rhonda."

"Hi, Rhonda—my name's Kathy," she said.

Rhonda smiled at her. "Hullo, Kathy. Are you staying in Fieldville long?" she asked.

Kathy stopped for a minute. "I hadn't really thought about that. I'm just looking for a place on my own, right now. You know—a fresh start. I'm not sure where that will be, exactly."

Rhonda nodded in acknowledgment. "Oh. Well, I hope to see you again. If you're planning on staying, you'll need groceries." She paused, then added, "I own a grocery store—Rhonda's Mart. I hope we can chat later!" She hopped into her car, "Bye, Doll!" she said, then drove off.

Kathy waved goodbye, then decided to look around Fieldville for a place to live. Her first impression was that life here could be great.

***

"Tom, in here!" she called out. "Tom, you need to see the bedroom!"

He walked into the room. "What are you hollering for, Babe?"

Katie turned around, a smile on her face. "Isn't the bedroom lovely?"

Tom took a quick glance at the cream walls and huge windows. "Sure."

Katie failed to notice his lack of enthusiasm. She loved the open room with all the light flooding in. It looked so bright and happy, so pleasant to live in. "Oh Tom, let's live here"

They moved in ten weeks later, and the room was repainted ten days later. Her first impression of life in that house had been wrong. Was she wrong again?

Chapter 15

LITTLE PINK HOUSES

Kathy pulled up in front of a small pink house with white trim. The porch had a broken swing that hung sideways, the garden needed replanting, and the paint was chipped. But it looked like such a cosy cottage that Kathy couldn't help wanting to check it out. Something about it drew her in. She looked at the For Rent sign one last time before getting out of her car and walking up the stone path.

A woman named Linda owned the house. Like Rhonda, she was very cheerful, and she was happy to show Kathy it on such short notice.

The house was small—kitchen and an adjoining dining area with a round, white table and two chairs, and a small living room with just enough room for a couch and a recliner around a coffee table with an empty vase on it. The only bedroom and bath were upstairs in the attic.

"The house was a seasonal rental property."

"Pardon? Oh, sorry, Linda—I was just thinking how perfect it is." *And how much Tom would have hated it.* The thought made her smile.

"Yeah, it's great," Linda said, looking around mournfully. She shook her head. "As I was saying, it was a seasonal rental. My husband and I kept it running, but we're just too on the go. So we decided to get someone for all year round." To whet Kathy's interest, she added, "Furnished, and all inclusive." Kathy stared at her for a second; she really did like this house. "With the kids, and our full-time jobs, we just don't have the time anymore. We had a few teenagers before and they caused a lot of problems. You'd be doing us a huge favour."

"I'll take it." Kathy said, smiling.

Linda smiled back, looking relieved. "How soon can you move in?"

Kathy let out a small laugh. "As soon as possible."

Chapter 16

A VISITOR FROM THE PAST

That night Kathy lay in her new bed, in her new house, in a new town, excited about starting over. Unfortunately, she didn't sleep well, and tossed and turned for hours before falling asleep.

In the middle of the night she woke with a start. There was a noise, a creak. "There are bound to be noises I'm not used to in an unfamiliar house," she said to herself. She heard it again—a long, drawn-out creeeeeaaaaak. She grabbed a flashlight from the nightstand, got up, and crept down the stairs.

The beam from her flashlight was a small pool of light in front of her. The noise was coming from the dining room. "H-hello?" she squeaked out, "Is an-anyone there?" The noise stopped, and a figure froze before her. A man! A *man* was in her house! She heard a gun cock. "Go back to bed." Kathy tried to move but couldn't. "I said, go back to bed, *Katie*!"

His voice came through loud and clear, and she recognized it immediately. "T-Tom?" she stammered.

"That's right, Honey," he said with a cruel laugh, "I'm home."

Kathy was confused. *This makes no sense. What's going on?* She found her voice. "No—I stabbed you, with the glass." She shook her head. "You're dead!" She shined the light in his angry face. It *was* him!

He smiled. "No, I could never leave you. But you, on the other hand . . ." He raised the gun.

"Tom, please, please don't," she begged.

"Shut up, Katie! Why do you always have to interrupt me?" He sighed heavily. "Now, where was I? Oh, yes." He chuckled. "I could never leave you—but you, on the other hand . . . You thought you could leave me, and now you're going on a permanent trip. You, my dear, are going away, for good!" Kathy screamed as three shots fired and she dropped her flashlight.

Kathy sat straight up in bed, awakened by her scream. She tried to catch her breath. "It was just a dream—he can't hurt me anymore!" she whispered.

That's when she heard a noise from downstairs—creeaak. "Maybe I'm just dreaming again," she told herself, trying to think logically. She pinched her arm and was rewarded with a very real pain. It wasn't a dream.

Chapter 17

AN UNEXPECTED GUEST

Maybe it was just a noise in an unfamiliar house. But she heard it again—creak—and then a crash, and her body went rigid. She heard glass shattering and took a couple of deep breaths. Maybe it was the wind and she was just being silly. She did not want to live her life like this. The next thing she knew, she was walking down her stairs with her flashlight in front of her.

The sound was coming from her dining room. It was all she could do to keep from running back up the stairs and hiding under the covers. Her mind was playing terrible tricks on her, but somehow she ventured on.

"Stop where you are," she heard her own voice yell into the darkness. The figure leapt at her and she let out a small scream.

"Meow." And there it was—a small tabby cat. She let out a laugh. "Where did you come from?" The cat just looked at her, and she picked it up. He licked her with a rough tongue. Her breathing settled, and she carried her new, furry friend upstairs.

It was late afternoon when Kathy awoke the next day. Sleep seemed to be exactly what she needed, and there were no more bad dreams. The cat was curled up by her head. She'd decided to call him Whiskers. She knew it was a simple name for a cat, but having never had one before, she decided it was as good as any.

She went downstairs to the kitchen to pour him some milk. While she drank her coffee, she started to make a "to-do list." The cat coiled around her leg, purring, having finished his drink, and she added "vet's office" to the list.

"Now you stay here, Whiskers, and I'll be back to get you in a bit," she said, opening the door. But Whiskers had plans of his own—he ran out the door before she could shut it. Kathy laughed, rolling her eyes. He seemed intent on following her. "I guess you can come too," she told the cat.

Driving along the road, she saw her first stop—Rhonda's. "Now, Whiskers, you have to stay here this time. I'll be right back," she said after rolling down the windows a little.

When Kathy stepped into the store, she spotted Rhonda right away, talking to an elderly man paying for his groceries. "There you go, Mr. Butterkey," she said, handing the man a brown paper sack.

Rhonda smiled when she saw Kathy. "Hey, I guess you decided to stay after all!"

Kathy returned Rhonda's grin. "Yeah, well this town just seems so peaceful. I couldn't help but stay. I rented that pink house around the corner." Rhonda nodded. "My cupboards are empty and a friend recommended this place."

She smiled at Rhonda, who grinned. "Well, we do have whatever you need." Kathy nodded then started to look around. It was a weird feeling to pick out groceries just for herself.

***

Katie returned from the grocery store as Tom was getting home from work. "Can you give me a hand please, Hun?"

He walked past her as if he didn't hear and closed the door behind him. Katie grabbed two bags and struggled to reopen the door. Once inside, she set them on the kitchen counter. "Hey, Tom—can you give me a hand with the groceries, please?

"Katie, don't bother me now—I just got in the door. It was a long day."

She nodded and went back out for the remaining bags. After another two trips she was done. As she entered the house the final time, she saw Tom in the kitchen poking through the bags. "What's this?" he asked.

As she set down the bags and began unpacking, she looked over at what he held in his hand. "It's a can of pasta sauce."

"Don't be stupid, Katie. I know it's pasta sauce, I can read. I mean why did you buy this shit?" She didn't quite know how to answer, and she could see he was getting angry. "*I asked you a question!*"

"For spaghetti?"

He grabbed her arm and squeezed. "I didn't ask you to be a smartass, Katie! *It's the wrong one!*"

She tried to pull free, but he tightened his grip. "I'm sorry, Tom . . . please let go."

"I only like Ragu! Ragu comes in a jar. This is something else . . . this is in a can. *Do you think you can get it RIGHT next time?*"

She stared at him in disbelief . . . *Is this really happening?* She nodded.

"Good." He let go and pushed her.

The outline of his hand remained on her arm, and as she put away the groceries he loomed over her. Every so often she'd get to an item that he would declare to be the "wrong" brand. The handprint on her arm went along with every mental note she made of her mistakes. She'd try harder to please him next time. She'd get the right stuff and make him happy.

***

Finally she didn't have to buy things she didn't like but bought anyway to please Tom. It was a liberating experience.

After paying for her groceries and accepting an invitation for afternoon tea at Rhonda's tomorrow, Kathy returned to her car to see a happy Whiskers waiting for her. Kathy looked around at her surroundings as she drove to the vet's. The town seemed quiet, yet cheerful—and very friendly, as neighbours waved as she passed by. "I could really get used to a place like this," she told Whiskers. He just sat there and looked at her.

When Kathy pulled into the vet's parking lot, Whiskers was very calm. She carefully picked him up and carried him in. A young woman sat at the front desk, talking to a man in a white coat. They looked up when Kathy came in. "Hello," he said. When he didn't recognize Kathy, he introduced himself. "I'm Dr. Peter Namile. Who do we have here?"

Honey, I'm Home

"Well I'm Kathy and this is Whiskers. We don't have an appointment but I thought I'd see if I could make one."

Dr. Namile looked at the cat. "Hello, Whiskers. It just so happens that my last appointment had to cancel short notice. Please come in."

When they were inside the room, he turned his attention to Kathy. "And what seems to be the problem with Whiskers?"

"Oh, there's no problem. He just needs a checkup," she answered.

He nodded. "That's good to hear. How long have you had him?" he asked, looking at the cat's eyes and ears.

"I found him yesterday in my new house. He didn't have a collar, so I decided to keep him."

He nodded again. "If only more pet owners were like you." Kathy smiled. "Well, Kathy, everything is normal here. It looks like you have yourself one very healthy tomcat."

The colour drained from her face at the mention of her husband's name. "Tomcat?" she gasped. She recalled what Steve had said: *We had a few pets growing up . . . Tom took to hunting our old cats down and using them for target practice.*

"What's wrong, Kathy? You look like you just saw a ghost," he said.

No, I just heard one's name, she thought. "I'm fine."

"Okay, well a tomcat is a male that hasn't been neutered," he told her. The colour returned to her face. It was just a coincidence. Tom had nothing to do with it—he was dead. "And if it's a problem, you could always get him fixed," the doctor continued.

"Pardon? Oh, no—it's not a problem at all. Thank you, Peter." Embarrassed, she paid at the front desk and rushed out.

Chapter 18

MAKING CONNECTIONS

On the drive to her house, Kathy nervously clenched the steering wheel. *Get a hold of yourself, Kathy—you're being ridiculous.* She was a little shaky as she put away the groceries.

Kathy grabbed the bag of items she'd purchased for Whiskers. She opened the bag of cat food and poured some in a little dish. A few fell on the floor. She watched the cat eat it while she waited for the water to boil. "Looks like you like your food, Whiskers," she said. Then she poured some water over a teabag into a cup.

She stirred her tea. "I've never had this kind before," she said, looking at the package. "Says here it'll calm my nerves." Whiskers stared at her for a moment, then went back to his food.

Looks like I bought it just in time, she thought, *with that little scare at the vet's.* She shook her head at how she was behaving. *I'm okay now, though. Tom's dead.* She breathed a sigh of relief and took a sip. The tea was working already.

"Okay, Whiskers. Mommy has to go out now. You stay here and be a good boy," Kathy told him the next day. She was off to have tea with Rhonda. She tossed him a ball, and he stretched out a paw and batted it playfully. She was watching him play when the doorbell rang.

She walked to the door and saw the postman. She opened the door, smiling. "Hello Ms"—He looked down at his sheet—"Pegy?"

"Yes, that's me."

He smiled. "I have a package for you. Please sign here." Kathy eyed the brown box, then signed the paper. "Thank you—have a nice day," he said.

"You too, thanks," she said, closing the door.

She glanced at the time and set the package down on her coffee table, which was now empty, thanks to Whiskers. The crash she'd heard in the middle of the night had been the vase breaking.

Whiskers brought his toy to her, and she tossed it one more time before heading to Rhonda's.

"Thanks so much for inviting me, Rhonda," she said once they were seated and sipping tea.

Rhonda smiled. "It's my pleasure. Besides, sooner or later you have to meet someone here. Around here it's quite odd to not know your neighbours."

They laughed. "So why did you decide to come here? Not that we aren't happy to have you."

Kathy hated to lie, but she could hardly reveal what happened. "Well, I, uh, needed a fresh start. You know how it is when you, uh, end a marriage?" Kathy said, not lying too much.

"Oh, I'm sorry to hear that, Dear. What happened?" Rhonda asked gently.

Before Kathy knew it, she was telling the whole story, minus the part about Tom's death. "He was an awful man, he told me he loved me, and then"—she sniffed—"he'd show his love by hurting me. At first it was just yelling, telling me how stupid I was, but then . . . well, it got worse. I was too afraid to tell anyone—and you know, I just thought it was normal. So we stayed married. Then I found out he was cheating on me. How did I even get myself into that mess . . ."

***

Katie noticed Tom around school, but then again, who didn't? With his dazzling smile and wit, he was the most popular guy in school. Katie always found herself staring at him in awe, but she never had the nerve to say hi. Even though she was pretty, she was too shy to be popular.

She'd never had a boyfriend, but one of the guys on the football team had taken an interest in her and they'd been flirting. She was sitting on the bleachers watching a game the day she met Tom. He was also on the team. On that day, their eyes had locked. He'd smiled that famous smile at her and she'd blushed and looked away. But when she'd looked back, he was still smiling.

During half time, Katie's flirting friend came over to say hi. They were exchanging casual conversation when Tom came walking up. "Heeere's Tommy!"

Katie looked at him and smiled. His teammate glanced over. "Hi, Tom. Do you know Katherine?"

"If you mean this beautiful angel you're speaking to, then no, no I don't. Please introduce me."

"Tom this is Katherine, Katherine this is T—"

"Thomas . . . Thomas Beatrice," he said, taking her hand and kissing it. He seemed so charming and sweet, and her cheeks turned red.

His teammate seemed to be annoyed by Tom's forwardness. He tried to get rid of him. "Okay, Tom—see you later."

"Thanks, Buddy—Katie and I would like to be alone," said Tom, obviously ignoring the wishes of his friend.

"Ha-ha," he responded with a fake laugh. "Funny, Tom. Now off you go."

But Tom had no intention of leaving. He wanted to stay with Katie and get to know her. He gave his friend a light shove, and Bud shoved him back. Soon the two were fighting, and Katie stood at the side-lines wondering how in the world this all could have started over her. Two things changed since that fateful day; Tom and Katie were always together after that, and she never went by Katherine again.

***

Rhonda looked at her through sympathetic eyes. "Oh my gosh, Hun, that's terrible. How did you finally get away?"

Kathy thought about it. How to answer? "A friend helped me," she finally replied. Her heart ached as she thought of Jack, her beloved friend. She hadn't even bothered to phone him. It was too soon to call now—she wasn't adjusted, not yet.

Rhonda nodded. "It's good to have friends," she said in agreement, "I'm glad you're all right. Hopefully he'll get what he deserves."

He already did, Kathy thought.

After a lovely visit, Kathy rushed home to greet a lonely kitty. "Hey, Buddy," she said when she entered the house, and Whiskers meowed loudly. She threw him his ball and they played until her stomach growled. Whiskers stared at her, surprised at the noise. Kathy laughed. "It's just my tummy making noises," she said. "I'd better feed it."

He watched her as she walked into the kitchen, then followed. "Are you hungry too?" Whiskers meowed loudly again. Kathy smiled and opened up a can of cat food, poured the contents into a dish, and set it down. She then started on her own meal, and as she stirred her pasta, she watched as he pawed his food before eating it. Her stomach grumbled again, but this time the cat was concentrating on his food and didn't seem to notice.

After dinner, Kathy looked around her house. Ashamed it was a little messy, she started to tidy up. When she got to the living room, her eyes fell on the package that had come earlier. Looking over the box, she didn't see a return address. She shrugged and sat down on her couch. Carefully she unfolded the brown wrapping paper, curious about what was inside. When she got to a white box, she said, "I wonder what it is?" It was a little heavy, and as she was opening it a piece of paper fell out. She picked it up and read the bold print: "Welcome to the neighbourhood!"

"Oh, how thoughtful." Kathy smiled with delight. Then she looked inside the box and saw . . . a vase. When she pulled it out and got a good look at it, she let out a shriek.

Whiskers looked up sharply from his nap. The vase . . . it was the same one from home. But no—it had shattered when Tom pushed her over. Flashbacks of the fight filled her mind. She could feel Tom's hands on her neck, heard herself gasping for breath.

She shook her head. "No, it can't be the same one—it's just a strange coincidence." Whiskers pounced on her feet, scaring her. She let out a small scream, and the cat took off. "Oh, I'm sorry, Whiskers!" She got up and tried to coax him out from under the table, but he wouldn't budge.

She sighed and walked to the kitchen to make some more tea. Sitting down with it, she chewed on her lower lip. What should I do with this vase?

Chapter 19

THINGS THAT GO BUMP

A crashing noise jolted Kathy awake. She looked over and saw Whiskers attacking the box the vase came in. "When did I doze off?" she wondered. She smiled and watched her playful cat. The string that had once bound the box landed near Kathy, and she grabbed it. Dangling it in front of Whiskers, she laughed as he leaped at it. They played together, a welcome distraction.

The next day, Kathy was feeling ill. She decided to take some aspirin and lie down in bed. She wasn't sleeping very well, and even though the tea made her drowsy, there were always nightmares. Even with Tom gone, she saw his face, tasted his breath, felt his hands on her. *Why can't I just escape?* She tossed and turned before finally nodding off.

She woke when Whiskers licked her face and sleepily wandered to the kitchen to feed him. When she wiped the sleep from her eyes, she noticed the silhouette of a man looking in her window. When she rubbed her eyes again, he was gone.

The hairs on her neck stood on end and she rubbed the goose bumps on her arms. "Whiskers, am I going insane?" she asked as she looked out. She was like a child with her nose pushed up against a candy shop window. Her breath fogged the pane of glass as she laughed. "There isn't anyone there, Whiskers. Let's get you some food before I zone out again." But in her head she didn't find it funny. *There was a man there—I'm sure of it.*

That night as she lay in bed, she looked around her room, checking for shadows in her windows. Satisfied nothing was watching her, she dozed off and slept till noon.

Honey, I'm Home

"Rhonda, I just can't thank you enough! You've done so much for me already. This is beyond being a kind neighbour!" Kathy smiled at her friend.

"It's no problem, Darling! We need more help around here, plus you're a kind person. You're just what we need. I should be thanking you," exclaimed Rhonda.

They laughed together. Kathy stood at the counter looking around, waiting for customers to come in. She looked down at her red apron, fingering her name in embroidered white lettering. She smiled. *I belong here.*

After getting off work, Kathy picked up dinner, then drove straight home to be welcomed by an eager Whiskers. "Did you have fun while Mommy was at work?" she asked. Whiskers curled around her leg as she continued to talk. She wasn't used to living in a silent house yet. "It's such a nice day! Why don't we eat outside?" The cat looked at her as if he was trying to figure out what she said. She laughed at his puzzled look and opened the back door. Stepping out to greet the gentle sun rays, a curious Whiskers followed, ready to sunbathe.

It was hotter than Kathy expected. As soon as she finished her meal, she returned indoors to change clothes. Back outside, now dressed in cut-off jeans and a blue halter top, she relaxed in a chaise lounge. An ice tea beside her, she opened a book. After a few pages, she realized it was too sunny to read, She pulled down her sunglasses and stretched out. *I never had so much free time before! I never could have done this with Tom. He'd just complain that I was lazy again.*

***

Katie lay on the couch, box of Kleenex within reach. Hot tea in hand, she snuggled under a thick blanket. Flu season had caught up with her. The front door opened and she groaned. To make things worse, she'd developed a migraine earlier that day. Nothing was staying down, and there was no way she could take anything for it. "Katie?"

"I'm in here, Tom," she called out weakly, and followed that with a raspy cough.

"How are you feeling?" he said as he walked into the room and surveyed the used tissues piled on the coffee table.

"Not too bad," she lied, knowing how much he hated complaining.

"Well, you've made quite the mess. Is this what you do when I'm at work all day?"

Her cheeks flushed, or was that the fever? "Sorry, Babe—I'll get them when I get up."

His voice rose a bit. "Oh, no, please—allow me. You seem too busy." But he didn't touch them, just glared at her until she felt she needed to get up. Blanket draped around her shoulders, she picked up three snotty rags. She let out another small cough on her way to the garbage in the kitchen. She could still feel his daggers watching her. "So what's for dinner?" he said.

***

She looked over at the sleepy cat, who had dozed off in a pool of sunlight. "You know what, Whiskers? That's a good idea." And with that, Kathy took her own summer nap.

She was dreaming, and in the dream Whiskers was hissing at something. She peered through a light, trying to see what he was looking at. Struggling to see what it was, Kathy woke up. As her eyes opened, the face of a man shadowed over her! She tried to scream but she felt a hand over her mouth, then everything went black.

Kathy awoke in her backyard, very sunburned. She caught a glimpse of Whiskers still asleep in the same position. Puzzled, she sat up. "It must have been a dream!" She shook her head and laughed at herself. "I really am pathetic. Nightmares at twenty-five?"

She gathered her empty glass and stood up to go back inside. When she placed her feet in her sandals, her eyes fell upon the imprint of a man's shoes. She looked again, in astonishment. Was it all a dream, or was there really a man standing beside her as she slept?

Chapter 20

PARANOIA

Before going to bed that night, Kathy triple-checked all the doors and windows, trying to convince herself that if she got more sleep her imagination would quit playing tricks on her.

By morning, Kathy had forgotten about the occurrences of the afternoon before—or maybe she'd just blocked them out. Whatever the case, she was cheerful when she left the house for work.

"You look happy today!" Rhonda said as she welcomed her. "Good—we need some happiness in here on such a stormy day."

Kathy looked out and saw the storm clouds gathering. "I didn't even notice the weather when I left the house this morning."

By afternoon, Kathy welcomed her break. It had been awhile since she'd had one of those, with Tom always making decisions for her, making her think breaks were for those who didn't want to make money. She needed to be a pro, earn more. Freedom was not even up for discussion.

A woman sat down at the picnic table in front of the store. "Hello, Dear. Just wanted to see how you were doing, just moving here and all. Have you settled in all right?"

Kathy smiled at the friendly neighbour. "Yes, although I'm not used to it yet. It's a really nice place."

The woman stuck out her hand. "I'm Maddy." They shook hands.

"Hi Maddy, I'm Kathy. Thanks for welcoming me like this. Meeting new people is nice."

Rhonda had warned Kathy about Maddy—she was the town gossip. If she talked to you, it was because she wanted to know something. And right now she smiled like she knew a secret. Kathy waited for her to say whatever she'd come over to say.

"Yeah, it seems like you've met a few new people here, like that man that was over yesterday," Maddy said with a twinkle in her eye.

The implication caught Kathy off guard. *Man?* She cleared her throat. "What man?"

Maddy sat up straight, as if Kathy had suggested she was lying. It must have offended her. "The tall, handsome man that was visiting you yesterday afternoon."

Visions of the man standing over her flashed in Kathy's eyes. She didn't want Maddy to sense her fear. "Oh, him! No we weren't visiting. He was, um . . . a pesky salesman."

Maddy looked at her carefully. "Well, it wasn't the first time I seen him there. Always hanging around, looking in the windows to see if you're home"—Kathy didn't know how to respond—"either that or you got yourself a peeping Tom."

Later, tired from a long day at work, Kathy flopped down on her living room couch. What Maddy had said stuck in her mind like an elbow on a face. What if there was someone who liked watching her all the time. That certainly would explain a lot. She got up and closed the curtains. Maybe she was just paranoid. "I'm a prisoner in my own home," she said aloud. Thunder roared outside. A few moments later, lightning crashed. Kathy locked all the windows and doors and closed all the curtains before heading to bed. "I'm just paranoid. Nothing is going on."

Chapter 21

GIRL, INTERRUPTED

That night, Kathy tossed and turned. Stress had set in, and she couldn't sleep properly. It seemed every time she closed her eyes, visions of Tom crept in. He was eating away at the candy-coated meaning of sweet dreams. Most frequent was the dream that had haunted her the first night. She saw their fights over and over, every time ending in her death.

Morning found Kathy still exhausted as dark circles took up permanent residence under her eyes. She was a mess, but she still put in hours at work. She skipped meals and would have been dehydrated had it not been for the stress-relief tea. Rhonda kept asking if she was okay. Not wanting to admit her torment, for fear of seeming silly, Kathy suffered in silence.

A month after escaping Tom and her past life, Kathy found once again that she didn't recognize herself. Once a beautiful woman looked back at her in the mirror, but she'd lost weight and her skin had lost its peaches-and-cream glow, with dark circles under what used to be bright, youthful eyes. Kathy had given up on her appearance. She hardly brushed her hair, just left it in a ratty old ponytail. She had developed a tremor in her hands. She swore she heard people whispering about her. Things did not look bright.

Then one day at work, things looked as if they might change. Rhonda was helping a customer find something while Kathy was shelving cans of corn. Out of the corner of her eye she saw a handsome man watching her. He smiled at her and she blushed, trying not to notice him.

Rhonda was saying goodbye to Michael Thomas when she heard Kathy scream. She heard the cans fall and could tell one had broken open.

She hurried to the window where Kathy stood looking outside. Her face had turned white and she was shrieking. Rhonda asked her what was wrong, but only cries came out. All she could do was point, and Rhonda saw nothing.

By the time the police and the ambulance came, Kathy had stopped screaming. Rhonda closed up the store and rode to the hospital with her. Still traumatized, Kathy did not speak, she just grasped Rhonda's hand tightly. A few town gossips stood around the store chatting about what they thought happened. No one knew for sure, except Kathy.

The doctor said Kathy had a nervous breakdown and finally assured Rhonda it would all be taken care of, and she could leave for home now. Was there anyone they should call? Kathy heard Rhonda say no, then say something about an ex-husband in a hushed tone. She gave her friend a quick hug and told her to phone if she needed anything. Kathy did not respond—she barely blinked. Rhonda sighed and then left, hopeful that Kathy was in good hands.

The doctors at the hospital were much kinder than the ones at home. Of course this hospital was much smaller, so the patients got more attention. Wendy, the full-time nurse, would visit Kathy numerous times a day. Each time Kathy just sat there, looking out the window, looking for answers. She cooperated and took the medication they gave her, some sort of anti-depressant. She felt like it numbed her, but she was already numb. Cold and alone.

When the door to Kathy's hospital room opened, Kathy sat there. She didn't flinch, assuming it was Wendy, back for another visit. She was right about it being Wendy, but she had someone with her.

"Hello, Kathy? I'm Dr. Martin," said the woman. Kathy turned, then turned back to the window. Wendy glanced at the therapist, realizing what she was up against. Then she left the room.

"Kathy, I was wondering if you'd like to talk to me. Perhaps tell me what you saw that day at the grocery store?" she asked politely. "Maybe I can help you."

Kathy shook her head. "No one can help me. He's back."

The doctor looked at her puzzled. "Who is back?"

Kathy's bottom lip quivered. She opened her mouth as if to explain, then closed it again, leaving the doctor with more questions than when she came in.

Honey, I'm Home

Dr. Martin wrote down what Kathy said, then retreated out of the room. The patient had seen some man that day, and it had been enough to upset her. Now the police could start questioning people about a mystery man.

Kathy knew she couldn't tell anyone, or explain what happened. If she did, she'd have to explain that she'd killed Tom and now his ghost had come back to haunt her. She felt so alone; no one here knew what it was like. They weren't there when he was hitting her. She was alone then, just like she was now.

No, wait—there is *someone who knows everything.* A tear rolled silently down her cheek. Jack!

Dr. Martin came back the next morning with more questions, "Police have been questioning everyone around. Nobody was near the store to see a man hanging around. Could you describe him to me?" *How do you describe a ghost?* thought Kathy.

She tried to think of what to say and wound up not saying anything. She certainly couldn't go into details of her past. How do you explain something like that? <u>*Dark hair, dark eyes, about yay tall, sorta handsome—the ex-husband I killed.* *Yeah, like I could tell her that!*</u>

The therapist stared at her. "Did you know him, who he was? Maybe someone you knew?"

Why doesn't she just go away? The whole thing was beginning to piss her off. *I don't want to talk about it. Can't they see that? Tom is dead!* She thought he couldn't hurt her anymore, and now his ghost had come back to haunt her. Would this nightmare never end?

"Miss Pegy, this is important. Please tell me what you remember." Kathy looked at the doctor's kind face.

"He had dark hair and dark eyes," Kathy said finally. *There, Sherlock, now please just go.*

Kathy thought that perhaps such a meagre description would disappoint the doctor, but there was nothing else to say. But the doctor's expression showed quite the opposite as her friendly smile widened. This could be the breakthrough she was looking for! "Thank you. If you remember anything else, just let me know—and don't worry. I'll tell the police, and they'll find him."

This news terrified Kathy. *He's a ghost. How will they find a ghost—call an exorcist? Unless . . .*

"We're going to find the man who was bothering you," said the doctor, interrupting Kathy's thoughts. *No it can't be, he isn't back. Tom is dead*, she told herself over and over.

She faked a weak smile. "Oh, I'm glad. I'm just tired," she lied. "If you don't mind. Doctor, I'm going to lie down." Dr. Martin nodded and left the room.

Kathy brought her hands up to her face and she began rocking. *Ghosts don't exist—it's just a dream. When I wake up tomorrow, I'll be back home.* But she couldn't get comfortable enough to sleep. Instead she found herself staring out her window.

Chapter 22

LOVE AND MARRIAGE

She saw a family playing at a park. A little boy with a ball cap was playing catch with his dad. He backed up and tripped over a tree root when the toss was too high. She watched as he tumbled over. His dad rushed over right away and picked his son up off the ground. He carefully brushed the dirt off the crying kid, then tickled him until the tears turned into giggles.

Kathy saw the mother setting up a picnic for her family, her daughter acting as her little helper. Once the blanket and all the food was out, father and son didn't come right away. Mother picked up a brush and sat down, and her daughter sat in front of her almost immediately. She brushed through the young girl's long blonde hair, then with care began to braid it. Her daughter sat perfectly still until her mom had finished. She kissed her mom's cheek and ran over to her brother and dad to tell them lunch was ready.

The three of them ran giggling towards a happy mother. Kathy watched them eat, all sharing the food, passing it around, happy. After the meal, the kids ran to the swings. Husband and wife were left together. He kissed her cheek and thanked her for the food. He even helped her put everything away before they walked over to push their children on the swings. He rubbed her belly, and for the first time Kathy saw the woman was pregnant.

That was enough for Kathy, and she turned away. She yearned for what that family had—love. It had been so long since Kathy had felt real love—the kind filled with hugs and kisses, smiles and warm gestures. Instead, bruises and harsh words, tears and pain marred the love she'd known—not the kind of love a husband should show his wife. Love was surprises and caring words, not threats and fear.

The closest she'd felt to being loved lately was by Jack, but theirs had been too brief. Tom had made contact with others impossible, and now he'd come between her and Jack.

"I'll keep in touch. I just need to settle in." That's what she'd told him, but when would she truly "settle in"?

Her thoughts were interrupted by nurses outside her door. "We've found no signs of this man. Nobody's seen him, except her," one said.

Another said, "Dr. Martin wants to talk to her in her office—but you know her, taking the more friendly route?" The nurses giggled.

One became serious. "I heard it's the only way they'll let her out of here. Dr. Martin is really concerned because this mystery man hasn't been found." Kathy's eyes widened. *They think I'm crazy, a loon!*

She listened more closely when she heard Wendy's familiar voice. "Kathy will have no problem talking to a therapist. She's a nice young woman. I'm sure she wants to go home."

This made Kathy smile; at least someone believed in her. She wasn't crazy, and she'd prove it. She pushed the button to call the nurse, and Wendy arrived in no time. "Do you know when the food cart is coming around?" asked Kathy with a cheerful smile.

"Anytime now. Glad to see you're feeling better!"

The next day when Dr. Martin came for her regular visit, Kathy greeted her with a cooperative smile. "Kathy, I'm afraid I have some bad news. No one has seen this man." She paused to make sure her patient was okay. Kathy bit her lip at first, but that was half-expected. Then she nodded to let the doctor know that it was okay to continue. "I think it may be a good idea for you to come and talk in my office."

Kathy nodded slowly. "Yes, I guess that's a good idea. When were you thinking?"

"The earlier the better. Tomorrow, if that's all right with you."

Kathy wanted to go home as soon as she could. "Okay, unless you can fit me in this afternoon."

That brought a smile to the doctor's face. "Yes I could fit you in today. How about after lunch?"

Chapter 23

THERE'S NO PLACE LIKE HOME

Kathy could barely control her happiness, the first good news for a long time—she could go home! Waiting for lunch seemed like torture. She heard people in the halls having conversations, holding up the cart. She wanted to just run out there and grab the food.

After what seemed like ages, Kathy was sitting on the couch in the Doctor's office. "Can you please tell me exactly what happened that day Kathy?"

Carefully considering her answer, Kathy said, "Well I was stacking some cans and I saw a man standing over me, from outside. I smiled at him, then went back to my work. But when he came closer to the window—" She stopped. What could she say—I realized it was my dead husband? The doctor waited, looking at her.

When Kathy didn't answer, she gently pressed: "Do you remember what happened after he got closer?"

Now she'd dug herself in a hole. What to say? "Um, I thought I recognized him as someone I saw on America's Most Wanted." Dr. Martin didn't seem to believe this and gave her a look. "Well, I've been under a lot of stress, not really sleeping well either. I just moved here and, well, Rhonda told you about my ex. I guess I overreacted," she said, trying to pass it off with a laugh.

The doctor nodded—this she believed. "Makes sense. I want to make sure you sleep well. I'll prescribe you some sleeping pills. We've begun weaning you off the anti-depressant but I still recommend you take them for a bit. Take it easy though, don't go straight back to work either."

Kathy nodded. "I'm sorry I've caused so much trouble. I feel silly."

Dr. Martin smiled. "Don't worry about it, Dear. Soon you'll be home and rested. I'm signing your discharge paper now—unless you'd rather stay for a bit."

Kathy was ecstatic. Finally she could go home. She shook her head. She wanted to go home more than anything, and "settle in." Her mind wandered back to Jack.

When she returned to her hospital room, she dialled his number. "Hullo?" said a gruff voice. Maybe Jack had found a boyfriend.

"Is Jack there, please?"

There was an awkward silence. "No, you must have the wrong number." *Oops*, she thought as she hung up. She dialled again, carefully. "Hullo?" It was the same gruff voice!

She asked for Jack Green this time. "No, he doesn't live here." She asked if she had the right number, explaining her old friend lived there. "Oh, he doesn't live here anymore. Sorry."

"Can you tell me"—the man hung up—"where he is?" Hmm.

She was about to phone the operator when there was a knock at the door. "Hey Kathy! I heard you get to leave. That's great," exclaimed Wendy, smiling warmly. "I just came to tell you, you're free to go now—and here are your sleeping pills."

Kathy returned the smile. "Thanks, Wendy. And thanks for trying to cheer me up."

As she left the hospital, she heard the same nurses talking. "You mean he came forward? She wasn't crazy!?"

There were a few whispers, then one spoke up. "Actually, who knows. She told people he had dark hair and dark eyes. The man that came forward was blonde with blue!" More whispering.

Kathy's eyes widened! She hurried past them and out the door. *I know it was Tom! I saw him! What if I am going crazy.*

It felt good to be in the safety of her home again. Whiskers was very happy to see her. She noticed there was food in his dish, and there were empty tins in the trash. "Oh, did Rhonda keep you fed? You lucky boy."

It was so nice to have friends she could count on. That reminded her of Jack. *I wonder where he moved to. Makes sense not wanting to be near where it happened*, she thought.

Chapter 24

HAPPY ENDING

After eating, she dialled 411. "Hi, I need the number and address for Mr. Jack Green, please."

She waited a moment. "I'm sorry, there seems to be a problem with our system. Try again later."

Oh, well—she was really tired anyway, and she and Jack had a lot of catching up to do. She took a sleeping pill and happily slept without a nightmare. In fact she overslept and only woke when the afternoon sun was shining in her eyes. Looking at the clock, she saw it was almost 1:30. It was so refreshing to get a nice rest.

She phoned Rhonda to tell her she'd be back to work in five days. Hopefully by then everyone would have forgotten her embarrassing misunderstanding. She got the answering machine, so she left a message.

Looking out the window, she noticed how nice a day it was. She wasn't about to spend it inside. "I think I'll walk to the mall! I haven't been shopping for clothes for ages!" Kathy spent the day hitting all her favourite stores—including McDonald's for lunch.

"Ready, Whiskers? This is my going-to-the-library outfit." She was back at home, and Whiskers was getting a fashion show of all her new purchases. Only he wasn't watching, he was too busy playing with new cat toys.

She changed into her pyjamas, heated a TV dinner, and sat down to watch one of her favourite movies. Following dinner came buttered popcorn.

Before bed, she reflected on her day. "I've never had a day like this! Tom would've killed me!"

But around four or five, her familiar nightmare struck again though. Just like the many times before, she carefully climbed down the stairs and shined her flashlight at the noise. And this time it felt different. After feeling so free today, she realized she could be happy and Tom couldn't get her. "You can't hurt me, Tom!" she yelled into the dark.

"I beg to differ," he replied. The dream followed her new scenario. "I know you still need me, Katie," he said with a cold laugh that almost sounded real.

But she wasn't giving up, "No I don't, Tom. I have my own house, my own friends, my own job, and my own life! What I don't need is you pushing me around!"

He got angry. "If it isn't true," he said, taking a step closer, "then why do you keep seeing me everywhere? Face it, Katie—you want me, you still need me!"

Arrgh, he's making me mad, she thought. She brought up her hand to slap him, but he was quicker. He thrust it back and slapped her. Katie didn't know what hurt worse, the pain on her face or the realization it wasn't a dream.

He noticed the shocked look on her face. "What's the matter, Katie? You finally woke up?"

"T-Tom . . . I don't get it." Suddenly her bravery abandoned her. "I stabbed you! You died!"

He shook his head and shoved her backwards. "That colour really doesn't suit you, Dear. If you'd stuck around long enough, you'd have known I wasn't dead. Badly injured though, thanks to you. But I followed you."

He knelt down to where she lay on the floor. "I think you look very sexy with brown hair," he said, rubbing his hand across her cheek.

She slid away. "I wish I had killed you," she said bitterly as she glared at him.

Tom stood, shaking his head. "See, that's the problem, Hun. I was willing to forgive you for the whole trying-to-kill-me thing, but it seems you aren't interested." He pulled a gun out of his jacket pocket. "You should have stabbed me harder." Then gunshots rang out.

At 7:30 a.m. the phone rang. When no one answered, the machine picked up. "Miss Pegy? We regret to inform you that Jack Green passed away weeks ago. We couldn't release that information until the family had been notified and identified the body. He drowned in the river near his house."

But Katie did not hear the message—she had stopped breathing and was laying still on the living room floor.

FOR ASSISTANCE

Even though this story is fiction, spousal abuse is real. If you or someone you know is a victim of spousal abuse, please know there is help out there.

Canada: call the National Domestic Violence Hotline at 1-800-363-9010

USA: call the National Domestic Violence Hotline at 1-800-799-7233 (SAFE) or visit http://www.thehotline.org

UK: call Women's Aid at 0808 2000 247 or visit http://www.womensaid.org.uk

Australia: call 1800RESPECT at 1800 737 732 or visit http://www.1800respect.org.au

Worldwide: visit the International Directory of Domestic Violence Agencies for a global list of helplines, shelters, and crisis centres at http://www.hotpeachpages.net

CPSIA information can be obtained at www.ICGtesting.com
Printed in the USA
LVOW080619300513

336031LV00003B/38/P

9 781622 122226